MW00906753

Five-Minute Peppa Stories

SCHOLASTIC INC.

Published by arrangement with Entertainment One and Ladybird Books, A Penguin Company. This book is based on the TV series *Peppa Pig*.

Peppa Pig is created by Neville Astley and Mark Baker. Peppa Pig © Astley Baker Davies Ltd/Entertainment One UK Ltd 2003.

ISBN 978-1-338-05804-8

10 9 8 7 6 5 4 3 2 1 17 18 19 20 21

Printed in Dongguan, China 95

First printing 2017
www.peppapig.com
Cover design by Becky James

Table of Contents

The Tooth Fairy 3

George's New Balloon 27

Peppa Plays Soccer 51

Peppa's New Neighbors 75

Dentist Trip 99

Let's Go Shopping, Peppa 123

Sports Day 145

Bedtime for Peppa 169

The Tooth Fairy

Once upon a time, there was a clever little pig named Peppa. She was very proud of her teeth.

Peppa and her brother, George, knew how to take care of their teeth. They brushed them every morning AND every evening!

Peppa and George loved playing dentist. Peppa would pretend to be the dentist and George would be her assistant.

George's toy dinosaur was the patient.

"What lovely, clean teeth you have, Mr. Dinosaur." Peppa smiled.

"Grr!" said George.

One day, after playing their dentist game, Peppa and George were eating their dinner. Suddenly, something fell onto Peppa's plate.

Clatter! Clatter!

It made Peppa JUMP!

"What's that?" she asked.

"Ho! Ho! It's a tooth." Daddy Pig laughed.

"But where is it from?" asked Peppa.

"Why don't you look in the mirror?" said Mummy Pig.

Peppa looked. She had a BIG gap in her teeth!

"Oh, no!" Peppa cried. "Do we need to go see Doctor Elephant?"

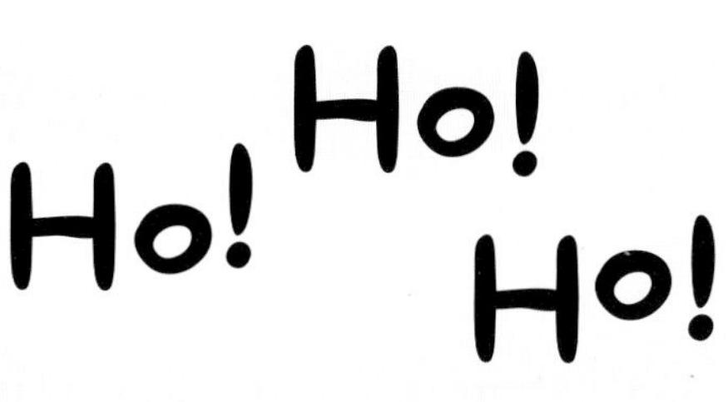

"No," said Mummy Pig. "It's just a baby tooth. It's meant to fall out."

"A baby tooth? What's that?" asked Peppa.

"A baby tooth is a tooth that falls out when you're young," explained Mummy Pig. "A new one will grow in its place."

"What should I do with my baby tooth?" asked Peppa.

"If you place it under your pillow, the Tooth Fairy will come. She will take your tooth and leave you a shiny new coin!" said Mummy Pig.

That evening, while Peppa watched television with her family, she kept thinking about the Tooth Fairy.

"When I grow up, I want to be a tooth fairy!" said Peppa.

Daddy Pig chuckled. "What about you, George?" asked Daddy.

George pointed at his dinosaur. "Dine-Saw!" He growled.

"Come on, George," shouted Peppa. "We don't want to miss the Tooth Fairy!"

They both ran up the stairs to get ready for bed.

"What are you doing, Peppa?" asked Daddy Pig.

Peppa was carefully brushing her baby tooth.

"I want it to be nice and clean for the Tooth Fairy," said Peppa.

Peppa tucked the tooth under her pillow. "Are you sure the Tooth Fairy will be able to find it?" she asked.

"I promise," said Mummy Pig. "Just you wait and see!"

"Good night, Peppa and George!"
"Good night, Mummy! Good night, Daddy!"

Hee! Hee! Hee!

Snore!

"I'm going to wait up all night for the Tooth Fairy," Peppa said. "George! Let's not go to sleep."

George smiled and nodded.

Peppa waited and waited. . . .

Snore! Snore!

She could hear something.

Is that the Tooth Fairy? Peppa wondered.

"George," she whispered, "did you hear that? Can you see the Tooth Fairy?"

She climbed down to look at George. He was fast asleep. It was him making the noise!

"I am much better at staying awake than George." Peppa sighed. She settled back in her bed.

After a while, her eyes started to close. She quickly opened them again.

"I am going to stay awake and see the Tooth Fairy," Peppa said to herself firmly.

Snore!

Snore!

But soon she was asleep.

Tinkle! Tinkle!

What was that?

It was the Tooth Fairy!

"Hello, Peppa!" she whispered. "Would you like a coin in exchange for your tooth?"

The Tooth Fairy gently took Peppa's tooth out from under the pillow and put a shiny coin in its place.

"What a lovely, clean tooth," the fairy said. "Thank you very much!"

Flutter!

Flutter!

Flutter!

The next morning, Peppa found the shiny coin under her pillow. "Mummy, the Tooth Fairy did come after all!" she shouted, jumping up and down.

"Oh, I wish I had seen the Tooth Fairy." Peppa sighed. "Next time I'm definitely going to stay awake ALL night!"

The End

George's New Balloon

Peppa and George are driving home with Granny and Grandpa Pig when they see Miss Rabbit's ice cream stall.

"Let's stop for ice cream," says Granny Pig.

"Why not?" says Grandpa Pig. "I think we deserve it!"

Peppa, Granny, and Grandpa Pig choose thei

ice cream.

George is next. "Dine-saw. Roar!" says George.

"I think George wants a dinosaur balloon," says Miss Rabbit.

"Alright, how much is it?" Grandpa Pig says.

"Ten dollars, please," says Miss Rabbit.

Grandpa Pig thinks the balloon is a bit expensive, but he buys it for George.

"Hold on tight to it," Miss Rabbit says.

But George lets go and the balloon starts to float away. Grandpa Pig quickly grabs the string.

"This is very valuable, George. I'll hold it on the way home," says Grandpa Pig.

Outside Granny and Grandpa Pig's house, George plays with his balloon.

"George," says Peppa, "this is an up balloon and if you let it go again it will go up to the moon!"

"Moon!" cries George and he lets the balloon go.

The balloon goes up and up but Grandpa Pig catches it just in time.

Peppa and George have gone indoors to keep the balloon safe.

"Hello, Polly," says Peppa. "George has got a new balloon!"

"*Squawk!*" cries Polly. "Balloon!"
Both Polly and George love the balloon.

"Oh no!" George cries, letting go of the balloon.

The balloon floats all the way out the door, up the stairs, and into the attic.

"Don't worry, it's safe in here," says Peppa.

"The only way out of the attic is the window," says Granny Pig. "And the window is always shut . . ."

But the window is not shut. The balloon escapes outside.

"Your balloon is going to the moon, George," says Peppa.

"*Waaa!*" cries George. Just then, Daddy Pig arrives to take them home.

"Oh dear," says Daddy Pig.

"There must be some way we can get the balloon back," cries Granny Pig.

"*Squawk! Balloon!*" says Polly Parrot.

Polly flies high up into the sky and catches the balloon string in her beak.

"Polly to the rescue!" cries Grandpa Pig.

Polly Parrot has saved the day.
"Hooray!" George cheers.
"Who's a clever Polly?" says Granny Pig.
"Who's a clever Polly?" repeats Polly Parrot.

"George, don't let go of your balloon again," says Peppa.

Daddy Pig has an idea.

"I'll tie the balloon to your wrist, George," he says. "That will stop it from floating away."

George is very happy.
He loves his balloon.

Everyone is happy his balloon was rescued.
"Snort!"

The End

Peppa Plays Soccer

It is a sunny day. Peppa and Suzy Sheep are playing tennis while George watches.

"To you, Suzy!" cheers Peppa, hitting the ball. Now it's Suzy's turn.

"To you, Peppa!" she shouts, hitting the ball straight over Peppa's head. Oh dear!

"*W*aaaa!" George feels left out.

"Sorry, George," says Peppa. "You can't play tennis. We only have two rackets."

"George can be the ball boy!" cheers Suzy.

"Being a ball boy is a very important job, George," says Peppa.

Peppa and Suzy are having lots of fun, but they keep missing the ball.

"Ball boy!" they shout together.

Huff, puff! George is not having fun. He keeps running to get the ball and he is very tired!

Then, more of Peppa's friends arrive.

"Hello, everyone," says Peppa. "We're playing tennis."

"Can we play, too?" asks Danny Dog.

"There aren't enough rackets for everyone," replies Suzy Sheep.

"Let's play soccer, then," says Danny Dog.
"Soccer! Hooray!" everyone cheers.

"We can play girls against boys," says Peppa.

"Each team needs a goalkeeper," says Danny Dog.

"Me, me!" shouts Pedro Pony.
"Me, me!" cries Rebecca Rabbit.

Pedro Pony and Rebecca Rabbit decide to be the goalkeepers.

"The boys' team will start!" says Danny Dog.

Richard Rabbit gets the ball and runs very fast, right by Peppa Pig, Suzy Sheep, and Candy Cat, and straight up to the . . .

"GOAL!" shout Danny and Pedro together as Richard Rabbit kicks the ball straight past Rebecca Rabbit and into the net.

"The boy is a winner!" cheers Danny Dog.

"That's not fair, we weren't ready," moans Peppa.

Rebecca Rabbit picks up the ball and runs.

"Hey!" shouts Danny Dog. "That's cheating! You can't hold the ball."

"Yes, I can!" says Rebecca. "I'm the goalkeeper."

Rebecca throws the ball into the goal, straight past Pedro Pony. "GOAL!" she cheers.

"That goal is not allowed," says Pedro.

"Yes, it is," says Peppa.

"No, it isn't!" barks Danny.

Daddy Pig comes outside to see what all the fuss is about. "What a lot of noise," he snorts. "I'll be the referee. The next team to get a goal wins!"

Richard Rabbit and George run off with the soccer ball while everyone is still talking.

"Where's the ball?" asks Peppa, looking around.

But it's too late! Richard Rabbit kicks the ball straight into the goal, past Pedro Pony.

"Hooray! The boys win!" cries Danny.

"Soccer is a silly game," says Peppa, disappointed.

"Just a moment," says Daddy Pig. "The boys scored in their own goal—that means the girls win!"

"Really?" The girls gasp. "Hooray!"
"Soccer is a great game!" cheers Peppa.
The girls agree!

The End

Peppa's New Neighbors

Daddy Pig is working hard.
He is building a new house.

The new house looks very small.

"Is it a house for elves and fairies?" asks Peppa.

"No," chuckles Daddy Pig. "This is just a model."

Daddy Pig shows Peppa and George a drawing of what the real house will look like.

"Something is missing!" says Peppa.
She draws a swing to go outside the house.
"Perfect!" decides Daddy Pig.

Daddy Pig takes Peppa and George to see the new house.

"Here we are!" he snorts.

"But Daddy," says Peppa, "there's nothing here!"

"That's because the building hasn't started yet!" replies Daddy Pig.

Mr. Bull is going to build the new house for Daddy Pig.

"Can you build it exactly like this please?" says Daddy Pig.

"But bigger," adds Peppa.

Mr. Bull shouts to his friends.

"Mr. Pig wants a house!"

"Is it going to be built of straw?" asks Mr. Rhino.

"Or sticks?" asks Mr. Labrador.

"Or bricks?" asks Mr. Bull.

Daddy Pig wants the new house to be made out of bricks.

Mr. Bull gets straight to work.

"Can we help?" wonders Peppa.

"You can lay the first brick," says Mr. Bull.

Mr. Bull tells George to put a blob of mortar on the ground. Mortar is a special kind of mud that sticks bricks together.

"Well done!" says Mr. Bull. "I'll do the rest."

Each brick must be laid straight and level. It takes a long time.

"Will you finish it today?" asks Peppa.

"You can't build a house in a day!" snorts Mr. Bull. "It will be finished . . . tomorrow."

The next morning, Peppa and George go straight over to see the new house.

"It's finished!" snorts Peppa.

"It's almost finished!" says Daddy Pig. "It just needs to be inspected."

Mr. Rabbit is the building inspector. He looks carefully at the new house. "Very good," he decides, "but you forgot the swing!"

"Oh no we didn't!" shouts Mr. Bull.

"Here it is!" says Mr. Labrador.

The house is all ready for the new neighbors to move in. Mr. Wolf and his family arrive.

Mr. Wolf tries huffing and puffing, but the house doesn't fall down. It is very strong.

"What is the new house made of?" asks Mr. Wolf.

"Bricks," replies Daddy Pig, "so don't even think about it."

Wendy Wolf likes the new swing.

"Can you push me?" asks Peppa.

"No," says Wendy. "I'll huff and puff you instead!"

Ha!
Ha!
Ha!

The End

Dentist Trip

Every morning, Peppa and George brush their teeth. *Brush! Brush! Brush!*

Brush!

Brush!

Brush!

"George, are your teeth as clean as mine?" Peppa asks, showing off her shiny white teeth.

"You both have lovely clean teeth. I'm sure the dentist will be happy!" calls out Daddy Pig.

Later that day, Peppa and George are at the dentist's office, waiting for their checkups. It is George's first visit.

"Peppa! George! The dentist will see you now," says Miss Rabbit, the nurse.

"Hooray!" they both cheer.

Peppa and George meet Doctor Elephant, the dentist. "Who's first?" he asks.

"I'm first," replies Peppa. "I'm a big girl. Watch me, George!"

"Open wide, please," Doctor Elephant says.

"Aaaaah!" Peppa opens her mouth as wide as she possibly can.

"Let's take a look," says Doctor Elephant, checking Peppa's teeth with a mirror.

"There. All done! What beautiful, clean teeth," says Doctor Elephant. "Now you can rinse your mouth!"

Gargle! Ptooou! The pink liquid tastes like bubble gum!

Peppa spits it out into the sink.

It's George's turn next.

George does not want it to be his turn. Doctor Elephant can tell he is nervous so he lets George hold Mr. Dinosaur.

"All done. You have very strong, clean teeth, George!" Doctor Elephant smiles.

"But wait! What is this?" cries Doctor Elephant. "George has clean teeth, but this young dinosaur's teeth are very dirty."

"The water jet, please, Miss Rabbit!" orders the dentist.

He uses the water to clean Mr. Dinosaur's teeth.

"Pink!" cries George, picking up a glass.
"That's right, George!" says Doctor Elephant

Mr. Dinosaur needs to rinse with the
ubble-gum-flavored drink!"

"Wow! What shiny teeth you have, Mr. Dinosaur," cries Miss Rabbit.

"Dine-saw! *Grrr!*" says George.

George loves Mr. Dinosaur—especially now that he has nice, clean teeth!

And now Peppa and George
have clean teeth, too!

The End

Let's Go Shopping, Peppa

One morning, Peppa and her family took a trip to the supermarket.

Peppa and George jumped out of the car in excitement. They loved visiting the supermarket!

"First, we need a cart," said Peppa.

Daddy Pig put George in the cart.

"Snort! Snort!" said George happily.

"Can I sit in the cart, too?" asked Peppa.

"Ho! Ho!" Daddy Pig laughed. "You're too big, Peppa. But you can help with the shopping."

"Oh, goody," said Peppa, skipping into the supermarket.

There was so much to see inside.

"Can we get one of everything?" asked Peppa.

"No, Peppa, that would be far too much," replied Mummy Pig.

"But how do we know what to get?" asked Peppa.

"We use a shopping list," Mummy Pig said, showing Peppa a piece of paper. "We have four things on our list today."

Peppa and Mummy Pig read the list together. The first item on the list was "tomatoes."

"I can see the tomatoes!" shouted Peppa.

Peppa counted four tomatoes as Mummy Pig put them into a bag: "One, two, three, four."

She skipped off to put them in the cart.

Daddy Pig crossed "tomatoes" off the list.

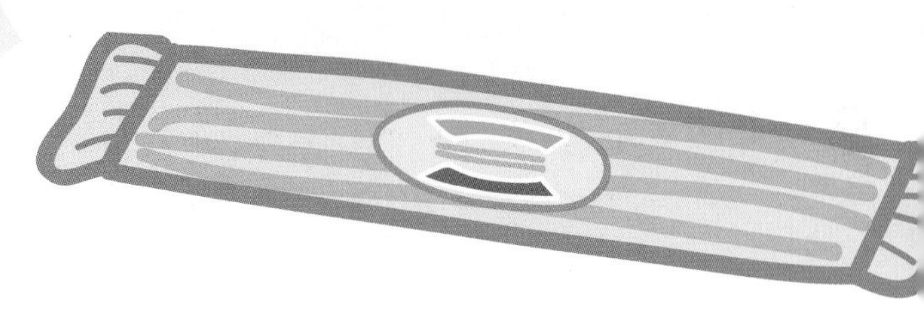

"What's next?" asked Mummy Pig.

"Spaghetti!" shouted Peppa.

"Pasketti!" shouted George.

Spaghetti was Peppa and George's favorite meal.

Peppa found the spaghetti and put it in the cart.

"Well done, Peppa," said Mummy Pig.

Peppa helped find the onions that were on the list, too.

The very last item on the list was fruit.

"I'll get it!" said Peppa.

"It's George's turn now," said Mummy Pig.

"How about **bananas?"** suggested Peppa.

"Or **apples** . . . or **pears** . . .

or **oranges?"**

George shook his head. He didn't want any of those. He wanted a **very big** . . .

. . . watermelon!

"Snort!" George was very happy with his choice, even though it was bigger than him!

Daddy Pig gave George the watermelon. It was very heavy.

George dropped the watermelon in the cart.

Rattle! Rattle! It was so big the whole cart shook.

"Hee! Hee! Hee!"

Everyone laughed.

"Well done, George," said Mummy Pig.

Daddy Pig crossed fruit off the shopping list.

"That's everything," said Mummy Pig. "Let's head to the checkout and pay."

At the checkout, Peppa and Daddy Pig put the food on the conveyer belt. Miss Rabbit scanned each item.

"Tomatoes." "Onions." "Watermelon."
BEEP. *BEEP.* *BEEP.*

"Spaghetti." "Chocolate cake."
BEEP. *BEEP.*

"Chocolate cake?" asked Mummy Pig. "That wasn't on the list!"

"Er," said Daddy Pig, holding up the chocolate cake with a guilty look on his face. "I thought it might be nice for dessert."

"Daddy Pig!" said Mummy Pig.

"Sorry!" said Daddy Pig, turning red. "It just looked so delicious. *Snort!*"

"It does look yummy," said Mummy Pig. "Let's pretend it was on our list."

"Hooray!" Everyone cheered.

When Peppa and her family arrived home, it was time for dinner. They had delicious spaghetti, followed by a big piece of watermelon, and a **great big** slice of chocolate cake!

Peppa, George, Mummy Pig, and Daddy Pig loved going shopping for food, but they loved eating it most of all!

The End

Sports Day

Today is school sports day. Peppa and her friends are all here.

The first event is running.

The children have to run as fast as they can.

"Ready . . . Set . . . Go!" says Madame Gazelle.

Suzy and Peppa are chatting about who can run the fastest.

Rebecca Rabbit is in the lead. Peppa and Suzy are coming in last.

Rebecca Rabbit wins the race!
"Hooray!" everyone cheers.
Peppa and Suzy are last.

"It doesn't matter if you win," Daddy Pig reminds them, "as long as you have fun."

"The next event is the long jump," says Madame Gazelle.

George and Richard Rabbit have to run and then jump as far as they can.

Whoever jumps the farthest is the winner.

"Ready . . . Set . . . Go!"

Oh dear. Richard Rabbit has jumped farther than George.

"Hooray!" shout all his friends.

George is not happy.

"Remember, George," says Peppa. "It doesn't matter if you win, as long as you have fun."

The next race is the relay.

Daddy Pig is in the lead. He hands the baton to Peppa.

"Thank you, Daddy. You did very well. Now it's my turn to—" begins Peppa.

"Stop talking and run!" snorts Daddy Pig.

Emily Elephant is the winner!
Everyone cheers. "Hooray!"

Peppa comes last.
She is not feeling happy.

It's the last event of the day—the tug of war. Boys against girls.

"The girls will win!" snorts Peppa.

"*Woof!* No they won't!" says Danny.
Everyone is pulling so hard the rope breaks!

The result is a tie!
"Both teams win!" says Madame Gazelle.
Everybody cheers.

"Hooray!"

"I love school sports day," snorts Peppa. "I had so much fun!"

The End

Bedtime for Peppa

One evening, Peppa and George are finishing their dinner. It is almost bedtime.

But the little piggies are not sleepy.

"Can we play outside for just a tiny bit?" Peppa asks.

"All right," says Daddy Pig. "But you must come in when we call you for your bath."

Peppa and George go outside to play one last game before bedtime.

"Look, George!" cries Peppa. "Lots of muddy puddles!"

Peppa and George like jumping up and down in muddy puddles.

"Peppa! George!" calls Daddy Pig. "Bath time!"

Peppa and George run home in their muddy boots.

Squish! Squash!

"We found the biggest muddy puddle in the world!" cries Peppa.

"Are you and George feeling sleepy?" asks Daddy Pig.

"No, Daddy," says Peppa. "We are not even a *tiny bit* sleepy."

Before bedtime, Peppa and George take their bath.

Peppa likes splashing. George likes splashing, too!

Ho! Ho!

"That's enough splashing," says Daddy Pig. "Let's get you into your pajamas."

"Oh, can't we stay in the bath a little bit longer?" Peppa asks.

"Bath time is over," says Daddy Pig.

Before going to bed, Peppa and George brush their teeth.

Brush! Brush! Brush!

"Okay, that's enough brushing," says Mummy Pig.

"Oh, but I think our teeth need a little bit more cleaning," says Peppa.

Snort! "When you're in bed, Daddy Pig will read you a story," Mummy tells them.

Peppa and George like stories!
They hurry into their beds.

When Peppa goes to bed, she always has her teddy tucked in with her.

When George goes to bed, he always has Mr. Dinosaur tucked in with him.

"Are you feeling sleepy now?" Daddy Pig asks.

"No, Daddy," Peppa says. "We need lots and lots of stories."

"Daddy will read you one story," says Mummy Pig. "Which story would you like?"

"The red monkey book, please!" says Peppa.

Peppa and George like the red monkey book.

So Daddy Pig reads them the story of the red monkey.

"Once upon a time, there was a red monkey. He had all sorts of adventures.

"After every adventure, this red monkey would . . .

. . . take a bath,

brush his teeth,

and go to sleep."

When Daddy Pig finishes the story, Peppa and George are fast asleep.

Good night, Peppa! Sweet dreams!

The End